Happy Cat First Readers

Duck Sounds

James Moloney

Illustrated by Stephen Michael King

HAPPY CAT BOOKS

For Jock Grant. *J.M.*

For Herbal. *S.M.K.*

Published by
Happy Cat Books
An imprint of Catnip Publishing Ltd
14 Greville Street
London EC1N 8SB

First published by Penguin Books, Australia, 2004

This edition first published 2011
3 5 7 9 10 8 6 4 2

Text copyright © James Moloney, 2004
Illustrations copyright © Stephen Michael King, 2004

A CIP catalogue record for this book is available from the
British Library

ISBN   978-1-905117-43-7

Printed in India

www.catnippublishing.co.uk

Instructions for Reading This Story

*To read this story properly,
you have to make a special
sound. This is how you
do it.*

*First, wet the
palm of one
hand with
your tongue.
Use lots of
spit.*

1

(Hold your hand flat, or the spit will run off.) Now get your mouth ready. Begin by pushing your lips out as far they will go. Make sure your lips are held tightly together. Bring your hand up close to your mouth. Press your lips firmly into the wet palm. Now, blow sharply through your lips. It works best if you turn

2

Quack

a little towards your thumb.
If the noise sounds rude,
then you are not doing it
properly. Try again.

If the noise sounds
a bit like a duck, then
congratulations! That is
just how it should sound.
You are ready to read
this story.

Chapter One

Jock was always the first
one in his house to wake
up. His two sisters liked to
sleep on and on, for hours.
What a waste! Jock couldn't
wait to start each day.
But he felt lonely eating
breakfast by himself.

Sometimes he would stay
in bed and listen for the
sounds of his sisters
stirring. Then he would get
up and have breakfast.

One cold Sunday morning,
he snuggled under the
blankets. There was no one
to have breakfast with yet.
The girls were taking
forever to wake up.
A train rattled by on

the tracks at the end of his street. Inside the house, there were still no footsteps, still no creaking of bed springs.

But what was that? Jock had left his window open just a crack, and a sharp squawking noise had just sneaked through the gap. He waited. Yes, there it was again.

'Ducks,' he said to himself. That was strange. He had never heard the ducks so early in the morning.

No, it's not time for our special sound just yet.

Chapter Two

Jock slipped out of bed
and went to the window.
He loved the view from
his window. Most children
can only see houses or
roads from their bedrooms.
Jock looked out onto a
huge park.

That morning, a thick
grey mist hung like milky
porridge around the trees
and over the pond in the
middle of the park.
The mist hid his view
of the ducks.

Sometimes he saw people walking their dogs in the park, but the cold had kept them away this morning.

Everything was still and silent. Then he heard that squawk again. Yes, it was definitely a duck.

He was out of bed already now. Sisters or no sisters, it was time to start the day. He dressed quickly in long trousers and his warmest jumper, then hurried downstairs to the back door.

Jock had his own private entrance to the park.

It wasn't a gate. It was a hole in the hedge he had made himself. He knew every centimetre of this park, every path, every tree.

He hurried to the edge of
the large pond. Out in the
middle, he could see one
duck, then two, three, four.
They were barely moving.

Just like my sisters, he thought. The same squawk broke the morning silence again.

But it wasn't coming from the middle of the pond. It was coming from the shore, from among the reeds and bushes hidden by the mist.

Sorry, be patient a little longer, it's still not time for our special sound.

Chapter Three

Jock went to investigate.
He had only taken a few
steps, when the mist rose
gently on a breath of
breeze. Now he could see
a man, crouching at the
water's edge. He was rather
plump and his grey hair

made him seem old. He put
something to his lips and
blew. A duck's *quack* called
across the water.

Jock came closer, until he was only a few metres away. 'How did you make that sound?' he asked.

The man turned around quickly. When he saw Jock was only a little boy, he relaxed. In fact, he smiled. It was a smart, unfriendly smile.

'See,' he said, holding up something that looked like a whistle. He blew on it. Instead of a shrill peep, like the blast from a referee's whistle, out came another duck's *quack*.

'My grandfather made
this duck whistle. You can't
buy one as good as this in
the shops.'

He blew on it again and this time the *quack* was answered. A little duck had come from the middle of the pond. The man blew again. The real duck quacked in reply and came closer.

The man stayed carefully hidden. He blew on that strange whistle again.

Quack

The duck came closer still.
Jock didn't guess what he
was up to, until it was too late.
The man moved like lightning.

His hand flashed out
through the reeds and
caught the little duck
around its neck. As Jock

watched in amazement, the duck was stuffed roughly into a canvas bag. Then a string was tied tightly around the top.

The duck quacked in protest.

But, no, it's still not time for our duck sound.

Chapter Four

When Jock saw what the
man had done, he was
angry. 'Hey! You can't do
that,' he cried.

The man didn't answer.
He was already walking
away along the path. Jock
chased him. Luckily, the

man had a large and heavy stomach, so he couldn't walk very quickly. Jock caught him easily.

This time, the man turned around. 'What do you want?' he asked rudely.

'I want you to let that duck go,' said Jock. 'It lives here, in this pond. You can't take him away. He'll be lonely without the other ducks.'

'You don't need to worry.

He won't be lonely for long,'

said the man, as he held up

the bag. 'By lunchtime he will be making friends with some nice potatoes. They can go swimming together in some gravy.' Then he smiled and licked his lips.

'You can't *eat* him!'
cried Jock.

Quack

'Oh, yes, I can. Duck is my favourite food. Too bad this one is so small. I was hoping for a big juicy one. Now, excuse me. I have to get home and put the oven on.'

Inside the bag, the little duck let out another angry *quack*.

Not long now. We will need that special sound, very soon.

Chapter Five

Jock had to save the little duck. But what could he do? The man was three times his size. By the time he ran home to fetch his dad, the man and the duck would both be gone.

Jock watched the man

as he turned away from the
pond. The railway line
blocked the way out of the
park on one side. He would

have to take the path
through the trees. Jock
knew that path. It wound
round like a snake.

He knew a quicker way,
and before he had finished
making up his mind, his
feet were already running.

He hurried through the
trees. He stomped madly

through the garden beds.
If the gardeners had seen
him, they would have shouted
angrily. But they were still
asleep, like the rest of the
world. Jock was puffing by

now, but he knew he was
ahead of the man and the
little duck. He pushed his way
through the bushes until he
was close to the path again.
Just in time, too, because he
could hear heavy footsteps.

What was he going to do now? His first plan was to jump out and snatch the bag. No, the path was wide and the man would see him coming. He needed to trick him somehow. What could he do?

At that moment, the poor little duck quacked loudly from inside the bag.

It was enough to give Jock an idea.

Get ready. We are very close.

Chapter Six

Jock quickly wet his hand with his tongue. In fact, he slobbered all over his palm.

Then he pushed his lips out, pressed them hard into the little pool he had made and blew a sharp blast of air. Out came a perfect duck sound. Just like this . . .

Okay. NOW!

The man stopped
walking. Jock could just see
him through a tiny space
between the bushes. He
blew hard down into his
wet palm again.

Right. DO IT AGAIN!

Quack

The man looked closely at
the bag in his hand. No, it
hadn't come from the little
duck he had captured.

Jock had to make the man think it was a really big duck, hidden in the bushes. He took a deep breath and blew as hard as he could.

Time for a really BIG ONE!

Quack

Quack

It worked. The man took
the duck whistle from his
pocket and moments later,
there was the squawk. Jock
replied right away.

*Again. Not so loud
this time.*

Quack

The man came closer, leaving the path now. Jock backed away with his lips still pushed into his hand.

It was time for the second part of his plan. This bit of the garden was overgrown with thin, curling vines. He snapped a vine from his left side. He snapped a piece from his right. He tied them quickly together with a strong knot.

By now, the man was
very close. He was still
hidden, but the squawking

of his duck whistle came
from only a few metres
away. Jock coaxed him on

Quack

with one last blast of his
own duck sound.

Last one. NOW!

Quack

He had barely finished, when the man leapt forward, hoping to grab a big, fat duck. But there was no duck. He broke through the bushes and all he saw was Jock.

The man's face crinkled
in anger. 'You again!' he
cried. He took one more
hurried step . . .

It was his last. The vines cut across his shins and over he went, like a huge tree chopped down in the forest. As he fell, the bag dropped from his hand. Something else fell free, too. In an instant, Jock snatched them both up and he was off.

Chapter Seven

Jock didn't follow any of the
paths back to the pond. He
had his own special ways,
so the man couldn't catch
him. In fact, the first the
man even saw of Jock was
when he reached the
muddy edge of the pond.

Jock quickly untied the string that sealed the little duck inside.

'Hey, don't let it go!' the man called.

It was too late. Jock opened the bag and held it upside down. The duck fell into the water with a splash. Then, with a quick

flap of its wings, it took
off to join its friends in the
middle of the pond.

By then, the angry man had puffed his way along the path to where Jock stood. 'It's no use,' he said. 'I'll catch another one next week, you know.'

Jock smiled and took something out of his pocket. He held it up for the man to see. It was the duck whistle. 'You won't be able to catch one without this,' he said.

'Here. That's mine. Give it to me!' The man reached forward suddenly, trying to grab the duck whistle.

Jock was too quick for
him. He took two steps to
the edge of the pond and
threw the duck whistle as
hard as he could. He had
never thrown anything so
far. It flew out over the
water. On and on it went,
until at last it landed, plop,

among the ducks. There
it sank, leaving a single
bubble to show where it
had been. Then the bubble
popped. The man would
never get it back now.

'But it was the best duck
whistle in the world,' the
man said. 'There will never

be another one like it.'

He seemed ready to cry.

Jock didn't care. He was glad no more ducks would be tricked by that whistle. He didn't want them to end up swimming in gravy, instead of this pond.

'How am I going to call the ducks now?' the man wailed.

Jock thought for a minute. There was a way.

He was about to spit in his hand, then stopped himself. No, this was one secret he would keep to himself.

'These ducks aren't for eating. Even if you buy another duck whistle, I will hear you. I live in that house, there,' Jock said, pointing at his bedroom window. 'If I see you trying to catch any more ducks, I'll tell the police.'

Jock turned and walked off. He climbed through the

hole in the hedge. When he
looked back, he saw the
man slowly walking away.
His shoulders were drooped
and his hands were stuck
in his pockets. Jock was
sure that the man would
never come back, but he
would keep a watch for
him, all the same.

He opened the back door
and there were his sisters.

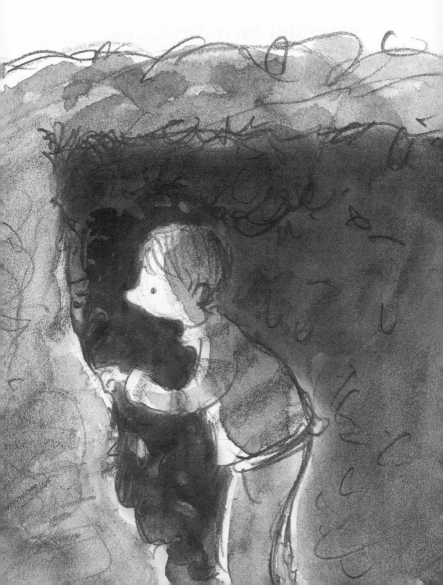

'Where have you been, Jock? We got up early, so we could have breakfast with you.'

Jock answered them with a noise. You know what noise it was, a duck sound! Then he sat down between his wide-eyed sisters and told them everything.

One Last Instruction
for Readers of
this Story.

You've got spit on your palms. Yuck. That's disgusting!
PLEASE WASH YOUR HANDS THIS MINUTE!

James Moloney

When I was in Paris one time,
I saw two old men catching pigeons
near a famous church called Sacré
Coeur. My French friend told me that
they would take the pigeons home and
eat them.

Later, I read about duck whistles in America. Some are hundreds of years old. They have been passed down from father to son over many generations. But when it comes to making noises with a wet palm, well . . . sometimes I was a naughty boy at school. I made noises like that at my teacher once, pretending that I was a duck.

Stephen Michael King

I'm often awake early. My daughter and Milli (our new dog), are usually up too. Quietly, we wake up Muttley (our old dog) and jump into our beach van. Then we drive towards the coast. We live in a rural area, so the short drive is often haunting and misty. Sometimes the beach is rugged and windswept, other times it's calm with perfect glassy waves. We return at sunrise, long before the rest of our family is out of bed.